How I Captured a Dinosaur

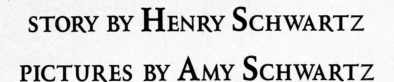

STORY BY HENRY SCHWARTZ

PICTURES BY AMY SCHWARTZ

ORCHARD BOOKS NEW YORK

A division of Franklin Watts, Inc.

Orchard Books, 387 Park Avenue South, New York, New York 10016
Orchard Books Great Britain, 10 Golden Square, London W1R 3AF England
Orchard Books Australia, 14 Mars Road, Lane Cove, New South Wales 2066
Orchard Books Canada, 20 Torbay Road, Markham, Ontario 23P 1G6

Orchard Books is a division of Franklin Watts, Inc.

Manufactured in the United States of America. Book design by Mina Greenstein.
The text of this book is set in 16 pt Schneidler. The illustrations are pen and ink with watercolor wash,
reproduced in full color.   10 9 8 7 6 5 4 3 2 1

Library of Congress Cataloging-in-Publication Data
Schwartz, Henry. How I captured a dinosaur/Henry Schwartz; illustrated by Amy Schwartz.   p.   cm.
"A Richard Jackson book." Summary: Liz, who is fascinated by dinosaurs, finds a living Albertosaurus on a
camping trip and brings it home to live with her.
ISBN 0-531-05770-4.   ISBN 0-531-08370-5 (lib. bdg.)
[1. Dinosaurs–Fiction.]   I. Schwartz, Amy, ill.   II. Title.   PZ7.S4077Ho   1988   [E]–dc19   88-1482   CIP   AC

To Eva, for everything

H.S. & A.S.

I first heard about dinosaurs in school. Our teacher, Mrs. Fegelman, showed the class a film all about dinosaurs. I found it very interesting.

So I got two books out of the school library on dinosaurs, and the more I read, the more interested I became.

I picked dinos for my science project. I made paper models of different kinds. Then I pasted a small mirror on a board to be a pond. I made some shrubs and trees and placed the models around the mirror.

I won a blue ribbon in class.

I asked Mrs. Fegelman if all the dinos were dead.

"Yes, Liz, they are extinct. But there have been some strange sightings of odd looking creatures...."

I started a scrapbook of these strange sightings. I found articles on Bigfoot in the Pacific Northwest and the Loch Ness monster in Scotland. Of special interest to me was an article about sightings close by in Baja California, Mexico, of a creature that stood upright, with small arms and a long tail.

It just so happened that my family had plans to go camping in Baja.

After school let out for summer vacation, Mom, Dad, and I packed our van with a tent and supplies and took off.

I told Dad I wanted to check out the sightings, and he agreed to drive to the area mentioned in the article. Since Mom gets easily excited, I just told her I was looking for dino bones.

We drove across the Mexican border and south into rugged country—canyons, mountains, sagebrush, and desert. Dad found a dirt road to the area I had pinpointed on a map. There we stopped to camp.

The next morning I went exploring. About half a mile from camp I made an exciting discovery. I found big footprints. They had three toes. I followed the prints to a small pond surrounded by shrubs. Here I found fresh prints, sunk deep in the mud. This looked promising. I decided to return after lunch.

Back at camp, Mom had cooked hamburgers. She made three extra hamburgers for second helpings, but only Dad wanted more. I took the two leftover hamburgers for something I had in mind.

In the late afternoon, when it wasn't so hot, I returned to the pond. I placed a hamburger on a rock near the water, and I hid in the shrubs about fifteen feet away.

I waited and waited. Nothing happened.

I was about to give up and go back to camp when I heard a grunting noise. Looking up I saw a creature with a large head, powerful legs, and two small arms.

The creature moved cautiously toward the pond, then stopped when he spotted the hamburger. He looked at it and smelled it. Then he reached down and picked it up.

He quickly ate the hamburger. Then he stood up and grunted again. He turned his head toward me. I guessed he had smelled the other hamburger.

There was another rock about halfway between us. So I
darted out and placed the second hamburger on that rock.
Then I went back to where I'd been sitting.

The creature came over and ate the hamburger. From this
close position I got a good look. I decided he must be an
Albertosaurus. From my research I knew that bones of this
dinosaur had been found in the area.

The Albertosaurus sat down on his haunches and watched me. He seemed to be wondering what I would do. I wondered what *he* would do if I took a step.

So I got up and took two steps. He got up and took a step toward me. I started to walk slowly back to camp and he followed.

When I got to camp, Mom was barbecuing hot dogs over the charcoal stove.

"Mother..." I said.

Mother didn't take it too well.

After I'd helped Mom down from the roof of the van, she said, "Liz, who is your ...ah...friend?"

"Mom, this is an Albertosaurus. A dinosaur. We can call him Albert for short."

"Albert?"

"Mom, he seems to like you."

"Does your...does Albert...like hot dogs?"

"I bet he does."

"Mustard?"

"The works!"

So I fed Albert two hot dogs. He grunted happily.

When Dad returned he didn't seem as surprised as Mom, although he couldn't get his voice down to normal.

Albert seemed content to stay with us. So we shared more hot dogs with him for dinner.

After dinner we had a party, since today was my eighth birthday. Mom had a cake with candles. And Dad had brought funny paper hats and party favors.

Albert seemed pleased with the party. I put a paper hat on him.

This seemed like a good time to remind my parents that they had promised me any pet I wanted on my birthday.

"Albert can sleep in the backyard," I said. "And we can take him on tour of the schools and make enough money to feed him."

My parents looked at Albert and then at each other. Dad
said, "We'll see in the morning."

Next morning Albert was still there. So my parents agreed.
They drove to the nearest town and rented a long-bed truck.

I led Albert onto the truck without any problem. We packed
the tent and our supplies into the van and drove back home.

Albert didn't mind Los Angeles.
He seemed curious about all the cars, but he was sort of
frightened by all the people staring at him.

Actually Albert is shy. So I made him his own private place in the backyard.

Once Albert was used to his new home I introduced him to my pals, but only one at a time, so he could get used to meeting people.

People ask me what Albert likes to do. I tell them that what he likes best is running through the sprinkler.

Second best he likes to sit on the front lawn and watch the cars go by.

I've tried to interest Albert in TV. But the only programs he'll pay attention to are mud wrestling and the Flintstones.

Mrs. Fegelman came over to measure Albert.

She loved my idea of taking him around to the schools. And the PTA even agreed to pay Albert's food bill, since Mom is always running to the market to feed him.

The kids love Albert.
They found something he likes even better than running through the sprinkler—

to be scratched on the top of his head.